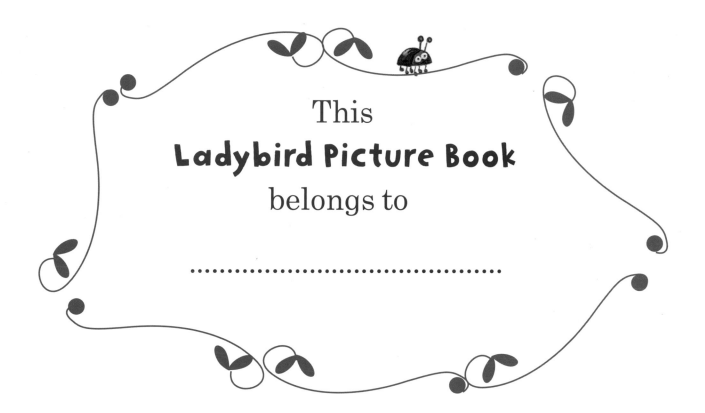

This
Ladybird Picture Book
belongs to

....

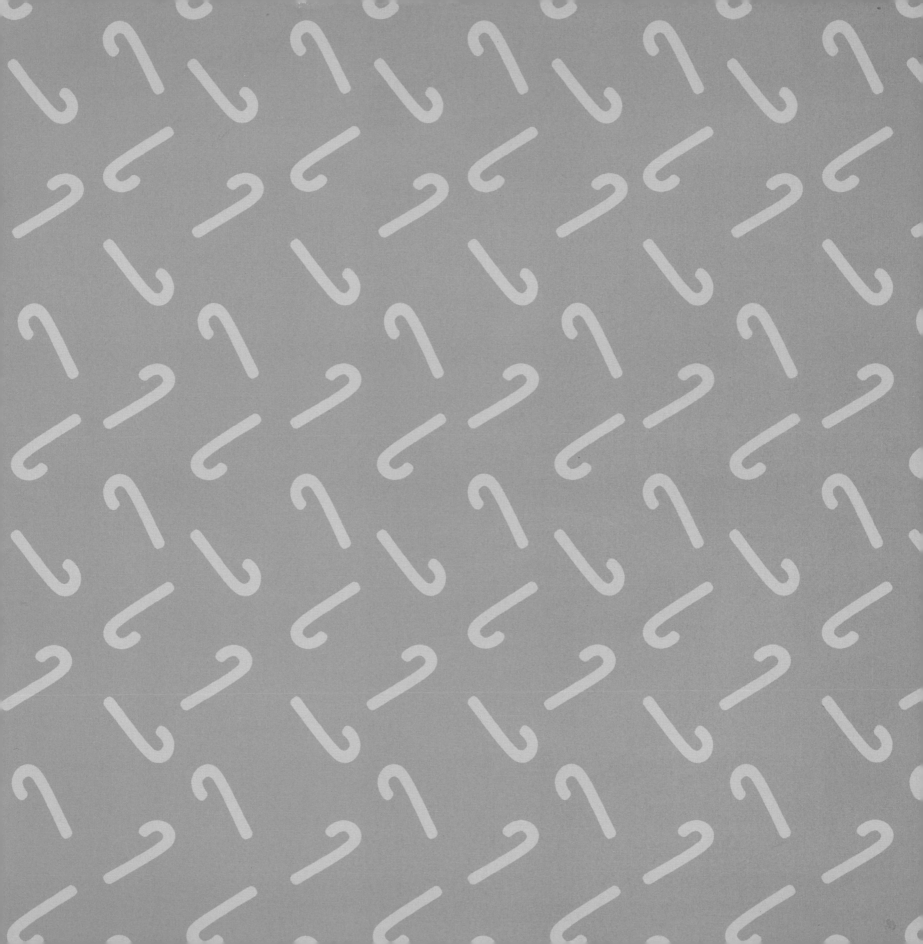

LADYBIRD BOOKS

UK | USA | Canada | Ireland | Australia
India | New Zealand | South Africa
Ladybird Books is part of the Penguin Random House group of companies
whose addresses can be found at global.penguinrandomhouse.com.

www.penguin.co.uk   www.puffin.co.uk   www.ladybird.co.uk

First published 2014 as part of the Ladybird First Favourite Tales series
This Ladybird Picture Books edition published 2017
004

Copyright © Ladybird Books Ltd, 2014, 2017

Printed in China
A CIP catalogue record for this book is available from the British Library

ISBN: 978–0–241–31538–5

All correspondence to:
Ladybird Books, Penguin Random House Children's
One Embassy Gardens, 8 Viaduct Gardens, London SW11 7BW

Ladybird Picture Books

Hansel
and
Gretel

BASED ON A TRADITIONAL FOLK TALE

retold by Ronne Randall ★ illustrated by Ailie Busby

Hansel and Gretel lived with their father,
a poor woodcutter, in a little cottage in a forest.
When Hansel and Gretel's mother died, their
father married again.

Hansel and Gretel's new stepmother was selfish and mean – the cruellest woman they'd ever seen!

One night, when the children were in bed,
Hansel and Gretel's stepmother said,
"Husband, we only have food for one more day.
We must send Hansel and Gretel away.
Otherwise we will all starve."

What will we do?

Father said no, but Stepmother said,
"They have to go."

Later that night, Hansel crept outside and collected some pebbles.

In the morning, when Father took the children into the forest, Hansel dropped the pebbles as they walked.

Father told Hansel and Gretel to wait for him, but he didn't come back. Soon it was dark.

But the pebbles shone white in the bright moonlight to show Hansel and Gretel the way home.

Hansel and Gretel walked all through the night to get home. Father was happy to see them, but Stepmother was cross. "Naughty children," she said. "I'll show you who's boss!"

She told Father he must take the children back into the forest and leave them there.

When Hansel went down to collect some more pebbles, he found the door locked.

The next morning, Father took Hansel and Gretel deep into the forest. He gave them bread to munch for their lunch, and Hansel used some of it to make a trail of crumbs.

"At the end of the day, the crumbs will help us find our way," he whispered to Gretel.

Father told Hansel and Gretel, "I'm going to chop some wood. Children, please be good and wait for me here."

But he never came back.

Gretel cried, "We're all alone!"
Hansel replied, "The crumbs will see us home."
But the crumbs were gone!

By the morning, Hansel and Gretel's tummies were rumbling and grumbling with hunger. Suddenly, just ahead, they saw a house made of gingerbread!

An old woman poked out her head.
"Come inside, my dears," she said.

But the old woman was a witch! She locked
Hansel up, and gave Gretel a mop.
"Do the housework!" she said.

Every day, the witch told Gretel, "Cook your brother some tasty food. When he's nice and fat he'll taste good – and I will eat him!"

Every morning, the witch told Hansel,
"Hold out your finger so I can feel
if you're fat enough to make a meal."

However, Hansel knew the witch couldn't see – her eyes were so sore and red! So he tricked her and held out a bone instead.

One day, the witch couldn't wait any longer.
"I'm going to cook and eat Hansel," she said.
"Gretel, light the oven now!"
Gretel replied, "But I don't know how!"

The nasty witch cried, "Just crawl inside!
Look, I'll show you how to do it right."
Gretel PUSHED the witch in and shut
the door tight!

Gretel unlocked the cage – she and Hansel could go!

But first they went round the cottage, looking high and low.

They opened a door, and – oh! What a sight!
They found piles of jewels, all sparkling
and bright.

Hansel and Gretel soon found their way home, where Father was waiting all alone.

"Your stepmother has gone," he said, hugging them tight. "From now on, everything will be all right."

With the witch's jewels, they would never be poor again. And they all lived happily ever after.

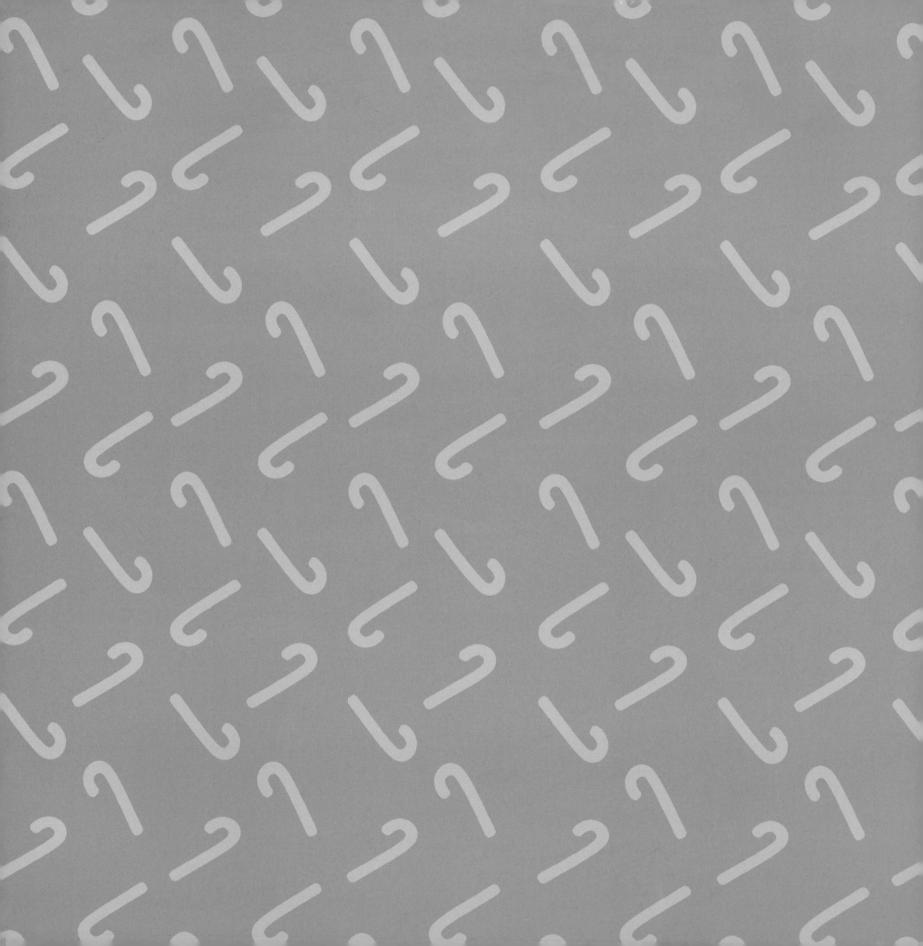

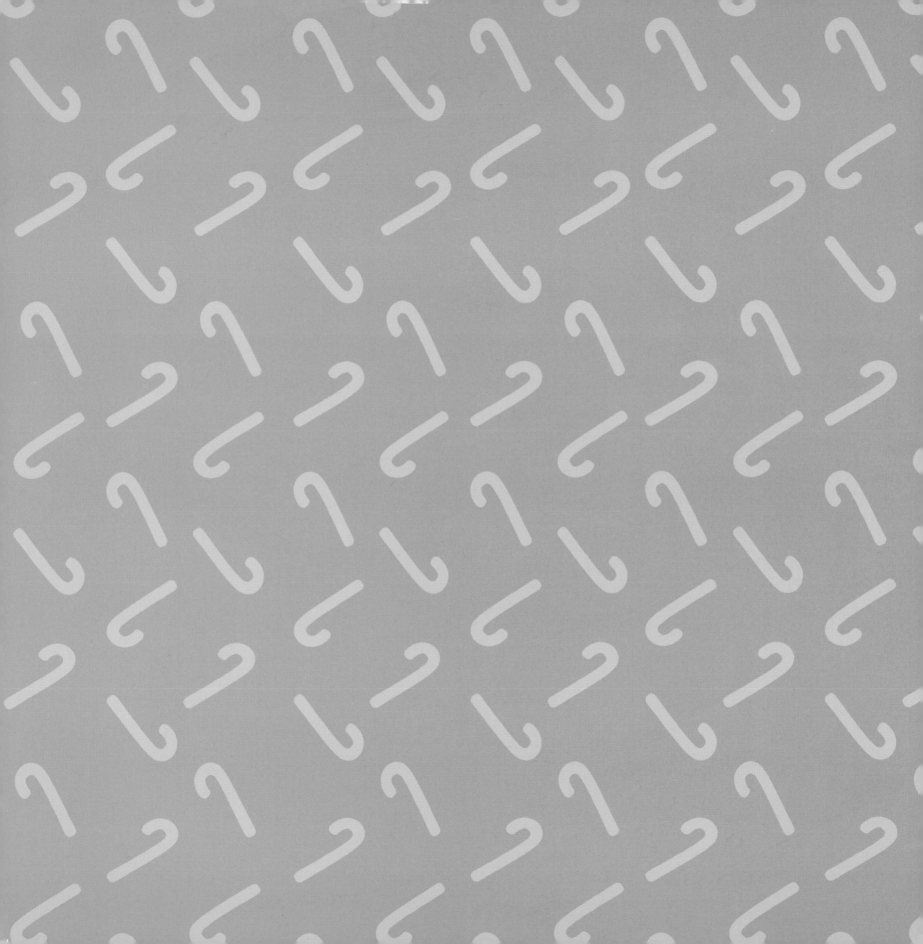

Ladybird Picture Books

Look out for...

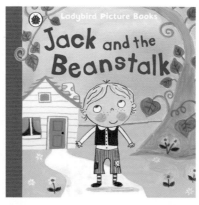

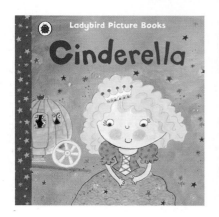

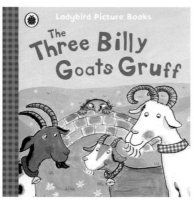

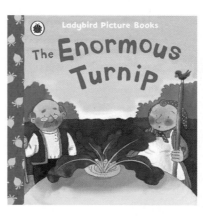

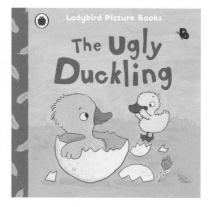

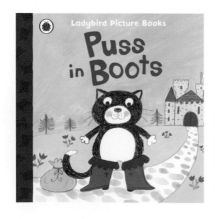

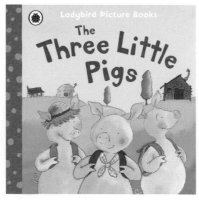